Miracle on 133rd Street

by Sonia Manzano

Illustrated by Marjorie Priceman

atheneum ATHENEUM BOOKS FOR YOUNG READERS

New York London Toronto Sydney New Delhi

atheneum

ATHENEUM BOOKS
FOR YOUNG READERS
An imprint of Simon & Schuster Children's
Publishing Division ● 1230 Avenue of the Americas,
New York, New York 10020 ● Text copyright © 2015 by
Sonia Manzano ● Illustrations copyright © 2015 by Marjorie Priceman ● All

bulk purchases, please contact Simon & Schuster Special Sales at 1-866-506-1949 or
business@simonandschuster.com. ● The Simon & Schuster Speakers Bureau can bring authors to your live event.
For more information or to book an event, contact the Simon & Schuster Speakers Bureau at 1-866-248-3049
or visit our website at www.simonspeakers.com. ● Book design by Debra Sfetsios-Conover ● The text for this book
is set in Aldus LT Std. ● The illustrations for this book are rendered in gouache and ink. ● Manufactured in China
● 0715 SCP ● First Edition ● 10 9 8 7 6 5 4 3 2 1 ● Library of Congress Cataloging-in-Publication Data ●
Manzano, Sonia. ● Miracle on 133rd Street / Sonia Manzano; illustrated by Marjorie Priceman. — First edition.
● pages cm ● Summary: The day before Christmas, everyone in José's neighborhood seems grumpy, including
his mother who is homesick for Puerto Rico, but when he and his parents return from the pizzeria where they
borrowed an oven to cook their roast, the heavenly aroma reminds those they pass of all they have to celebrate. ●
ISBN 978-0-689-87887-9 (hardcover : alk. paper) ● ISBN 978-1-4814-2892-7 (eBook) ● [1. Christmas—Fiction.
2. Contentment—Fiction. 3. Neighbors—Fiction. 4. Cooking—Fiction. 5. Puerto Rican Americans—
United States—Fiction.] I. Priceman, Marjorie, illustrator. II. Title. III. Title: Miracle on one
hundred thirty-third street.● PZ7.M3213Mir 2015
[E]—dc23
2014035882

JOSÉ was decorating the tiniest Christmas tree ever. It was practically a twig—and what was he supposed to do with the leftover ornaments anyway?

"José!" his mami yelled. Then she added a string of words he was not allowed to use— in English or Spanish.

José rushed into the kitchen and bumped into his father. His name was José too.

"The oven is too small for the roast," Mami said.

"We never should have left Puerto Rico. There we could have roasted it outside. Everything is too small here," she added. "Small kitchen. Small apartment. Small everything. We need a bigger oven."

"What we need is a pizza oven," said José, trying to make a joke. José knew his mother needed a joke; every Christmas she got homesick for Puerto Rico.

"That's not a bad idea!" said Papi.

They put the roast in the biggest box they could find and started out for Regular Ray's Pizzeria.

As soon as they closed their apartment door, Mrs. Whitman in 4B stuck her nose out of hers.

"What's all this racket?" she demanded.

"We're going to get our Christmas—" José started to explain.

"Christmas, Christmas, Christmas, that's all I hear all day. My kids are driving me crazy. I can't wait until these holidays are over and they're back in school!" And she slammed her door.

As soon as that door had closed and José and Papi had walked down to the third floor, old Mr. and Mrs. Santiago in 3C opened their door. "Is something wrong?" Mr. Santiago sighed.

"No," said Papi. "We're just going to the pizzeria to get this roasted for our celebrations—"

"We have celebrations," Mr. Santiago said, "when the children visit. . . ."

"But they can't come this year," Mrs. Santiago finished saying for him. And with that they closed the door softly.

That's how it was in that building on 133rd Street. Except
for Mr. Franklin, who only peeped out of his peephole.
"It's only us, Mr. Franklin," said Papi.
"Oh . . . ," whispered Mr. Franklin
from the other side of the door. "I thought
someone's television was being stolen!"

"No, no, no—this is our roast. We're going to the pizzeria to—"

"Are you nuts?! Going out on the day before Christmas?! That's when all the muggers are out. And it's snowing! You'll break your leg running away from them!" Mr. Franklin exclaimed.

Then they came upon the Wozenskys, who lived in 2B.

"Oh dear, won't roasting that cost a lot of money?" said Mrs. Wozensky when they told her what they were going to do.

"That's what I hate about the holidays," added Mr. Wozensky. "All the money you have to spend. Who has money to spend on a roast?"

Before José or his father could answer, the DiPalma twins ran past, Mr. DiPalma chasing them.

"Wait! You need your boots . . . ," he yelled, then paused long enough to remark, "Money is tight for me too; my taxi's been in the shop for weeks! It's awful."

"*I'll* tell you what's awful," said Ms. Simon from downstairs. "Shopping! I couldn't come up with anything for my nephews—I have seven of them. What am I going to do?!"

"Don't *buy* anything!" Mr. Wozensky said. "There's too much buying on the holidays. And the packages! They hold up the mail!"

The roast began to feel heavier and heavier.

Outside, José's best friend, Yvonne, was helping her brother,
Petey, take out the garbage.

"Merry Christmas!" José said. "It snowed just like you hoped."

But before Yvonne could say hello back, Petey barked, "Hurry up,
Yvonne! We still have to shovel the walk; we'll be here all night!"

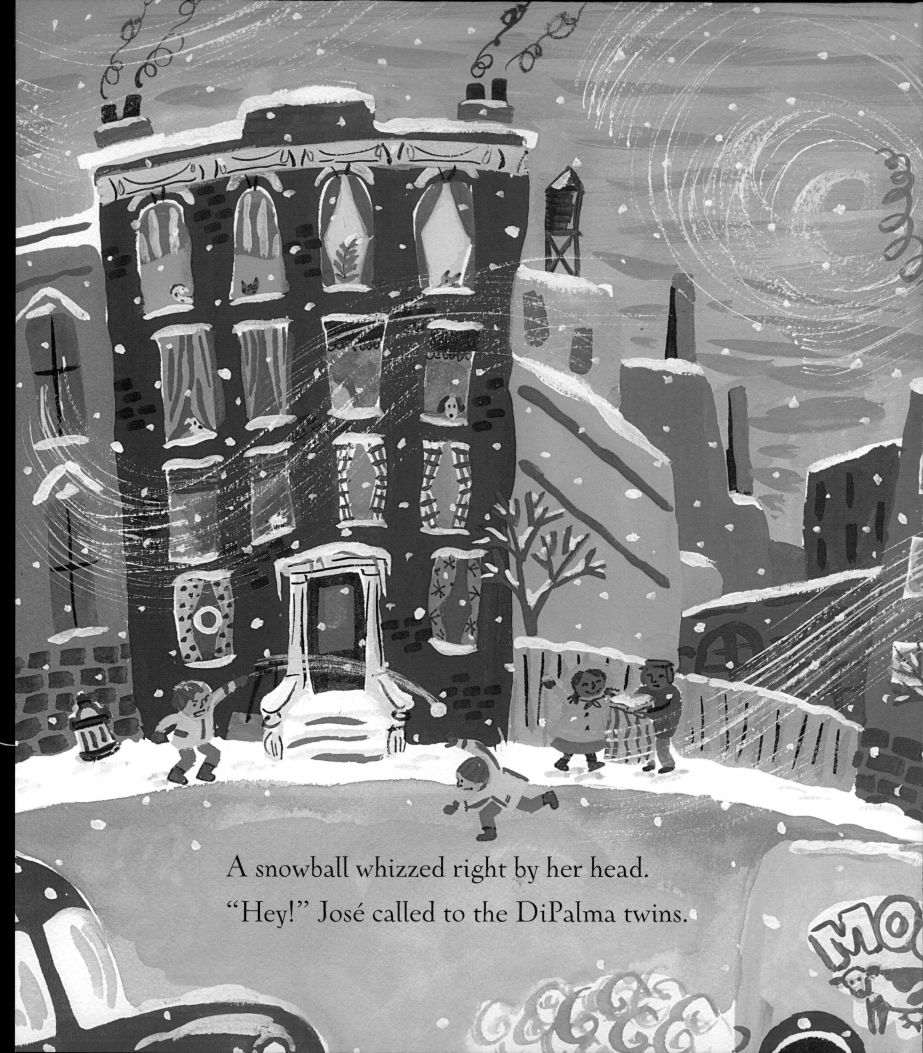

A snowball whizzed right by her head.
"Hey!" José called to the DiPalma twins.

"It's okay, José!" Yvonne said. "I love the snow."

And off José and Papi went, past the Happy Full Tummy Food Store (where Mr. Happy was making sure the price tags on his Christmas trees hadn't blown off), and over the Bronx River to Regular Ray's Pizzeria.

A bell chimed as they walked into the pizzeria, which was empty except for Mr. Ray. "Nobody eats here on Christmas Eve. They just take their pies and go home," he said.

While Papi talked to Mr. Ray about using his oven, José went to look at the Christmas tree in the corner.

"He'll do it!" Papi called out to José. "It should be ready in three hours."

José slid under the tree and waited . . . and waited . . . and waited. The next thing he heard was his father calling to him.

"José, wake up! The roast is done!"
And that's when it hit him. A scent.
A most glorious scent. A scent so garlicky
and olive oily and delicious it made you
want to eat—even if you weren't hungry.
A bouquet that made you feel excited,
except you didn't know why. A smell
that made you feel something wonderful
could happen, but you didn't know what.

The aroma seemed to lift José to his feet and wrap itself around all of them like a scarf. There was nothing left to do but hug. "Have a wonderful dinner. *Feliz Navidad*," said Mr. Ray.

"*Gracias*. But, why don't you join us?" asked Papi suddenly. "We always celebrate Christmas on Christmas Eve."

"Oh, but I have to mop the floor . . . and polish the . . ." Then he took a deep breath. "What am I saying?! There are no more customers. And it *is* Christmas Eve!"

He put on his coat and grabbed a package from the freezer. "Some of my cannolis. For your wife," he said as the door chimed closed behind them.

The snow had stopped. The sky was blue-black,
and the stars looked close enough to pluck right out
and put into your pocket if you wanted to, but
José decided to leave them just where they were.

His father and Mr. Ray waltzed on with the roast as José
floated on ahead until they found themselves in front of the
Happy Full Tummy vegetables and fruit stand. A customer was
arguing with Mr. Happy. "This tree costs too much money!"
she barked.

"It does not," snapped Mr. Happy.

"Well then, never mind!" said the customer, and she began to stomp away.

Then she sniffed the air, paused, and turned back.

"Well, it *is* a beautiful tree. And just the right size," she said.

And then the aroma formed a halo around Mr. Happy's head and *he* said, "Oh, just take it, no charge. It's Christmas Eve."

José and his father looked at each other,
then continued on their way, weaving and wafting
until they got to their building.

"Look at this . . . ohhh . . ." Yvonne took a sniff,
dropped her shovel, and followed them inside.

"Wait for me!" her brother said.

The hall filled with the smell of roast. Everyone opened
their door at the same time. "Is that a roast I smell?" said someone.
"*Sí,*" said Papi. "Why don't you all come and help us eat it?"

They knew the aroma had reached the third floor because
the Wozenskys and Mr. Franklin were standing in the hallway! Talking!

"Mr. Franklin, we haven't seen you in years!" Mr. Wozensky
was saying. "I was just thinking I'd run to the bodega to buy some
Christmas cookies before they close."

"And a cake would be nice," added Mrs. Wozensky. "A great big
fancy one. It's Christmas Eve."

"Why don't I go with you?" said Mr. Franklin. "I feel like
making a snow angel."

José, Papi, and Mr. Ray got the roast up to their floor.

Mami was already in the doorway, looking dreamy.

"Ooooooh, it smells like . . . home!" she said.

And before they could even get the roast into the apartment, Mrs. Whitman, her children, and Mr. and Mrs. Santiago were upon them.

"Please, come celebrate Christmas with us," said Mami. "We have a beautiful Christmas tree. And a huge roast."

"Celebrate Christmas on Christmas Eve, as well as
Christmas Day? What a great idea! The children will love it!"
said Mrs. Whitman, giving each a hug as she ushered them in.

"Let us get our guitars!" offered the Santiagos. "Our children
loved singing carols!"

Yvonne and Petey came bounding up the stairs with a few
extra chairs. "I thought these might come in handy," Petey said,
smiling.

As José, Papi, and Mr. Ray came through the door, the miraculous aroma filled up the apartment quickly. The guests filled the apartment even quicker.

"You know, this is the first time since the boys were born that I haven't worked on Christmas. *This* Christmas I can spend time with them," said Mr. DiPalma.

"Spend time with them? Why didn't *I* think of that! That's what I'll do—take my nephews skating in Central Park over Christmas break!" said Ms. Simon.

Mami looked at all of the people in the apartment and said to her two Josés, "Thank goodness this apartment is big enough to hold all our friends. It's a miracle."

Yvonne and José decorated the window
with the leftover decorations.
The tree was perfect.
And the roast tasted pretty good too.